for Pirates!

Raggedy Rocks

The Roaring Reef

Wicked Whirlpool

Mud Swamps

Spidery Jungle

Treasure Bay

Timber Bay

Parrot Park

Driftwood Dock

Skullabones Town

SKULLABONES
ISLAND

For Mum and Dad – **RD**

For my pirate crew Hannah,
Amber, Bobby and George,
who eat all their tea! – **SH**

Published by Ladybird Books Ltd
A Penguin Company
Penguin Books Ltd, 80 Strand, London WC2R 0RL, UK
Penguin Books Australia Ltd, 707 Collins Street, Melbourne, Victoria 3008, Australia
Penguin Group (NZ) 67 Apollo Drive, Rosedale, North Shore 0632, New Zealand

001

© Ladybird Books Limited MMXV

ISBN: 978-0-72329-419-1

Printed in China

Skullab☠nes Island

Teatime for Pirates!

Richard Dungworth ★ Sharon Harmer

The **pirate ship** bobbed gently
as a light wind whispered by.
Her crew, with tummies rumbling
heard their captain's welcome cry...

"TEATIME,
me hearties!"

"But Captain, what's **this** on our plates?

We don't want **this** for tea!

Peas aren't proper pirate food.

You don't eat those at sea!"

"**Tommyrot!**" the captain cried,

"Why, peas, you swabs, are **swell**.

Pirates **need** to eat their peas

to keep them fit and well!

They help when you feel seasick
or you're fighting Pirate Flu.
They'll stop you catching Pirate Pox
and fend off woodworm, too!"

The **pirate ship** sped smoothly
as a fair wind filled her sail.
Her crew, with tummies grumbling,
heard their captain's welcome wail…

"TEATIME,
me hearties!"

"But Captain, what's **this** on our plates?

We don't want **this** for tea!

Carrots? They're not pirate food.

You don't eat those at sea!"

"Carrots not for pirates?"

said the captain, looking gruff.

"**Fiddlesticks!** They're just the thing

to keep you strong and tough!

They give you strength for steering
or climbing up the mast,
for digging deep for treasure,
or for rowing extra-fast!"

The **pirate ship** pitched steeply
as a strong wind stirred the swell.
Her crew, with tummies growling
heard their captain's welcome yell…

"TEATIME,
me hearties!"

"But Captain, what's **this** on our plates?
We don't want **this** for tea!
Sausages aren't pirate food.
You don't eat those at sea!"

"Balderdash!" the captain cried,
"That simply isn't right!
A pirate **needs** his sausages
to keep him quick and bright.

They'll help you read a sea-chart

when it's hard to understand,

or make you super-sneaky

when there's mischief to be planned!"

The **pirate ship** rolled wildly
as a fierce wind brought a squall.
Her crew, with tummies groaning
heard their captain's welcome bawl…

"TEATIME,
me hearties!"

"But Captain, what's **this** on our plates?
We don't want **this** for tea!
Mash? That isn't pirate food.
You don't eat that at sea!"

"**Poppycock!**" the captain cried,
"Why mash is **splendid** tuck!
It keeps a pirate brave and bold,
and gives her extra pluck.

It helps when you're on lookout
in the crow's nest after dark,
or when you meet a ghost ship
or a hungry-looking shark!"

The **pirate ship** bobbed gently
as the wind once more fell quiet.
Her crew, with tummies aching. . .
staged a noisy pirate riot!

Bang!
Bang!

Ping!

Whack!
Clang!

Thump!
Thump!

"But Captain, what's **this** on our plates?
We don't want **this** for tea!
Sausages, carrots, peas **and** mash!
We hate them, don't you see?"

The captain only gave a roar,
   "By barnacles! Of course!
      I know what this meal's missing,
   I forgot the **Pirate Sauce!**

It's **great** with peas and carrots,

and with sausages, and mash.

There's no sauce **half** so tasty.

Don't believe me? Try a splash!"

Well, blow me down, with **sauce** on,

it was true – things tasted great!

And soon each hungry pirate

had a gleaming empty plate.

They felt like different pirates
    when their hearty meal was done,
Strong and fit, and brave and bright
    and ready for some fun!

So if you think that one day,
you might like to sail the sea,
and be a rough tough noisy pirate…

...then remember, EAT YOUR TEA!

Raggedy Rocks

The Roaring Reef

Wicked Whirlpool

Mud Swamps

Spidery Jungle

Treasure Bay

Timber Bay

Parrot Park

Driftwood Dock

Skullabones Town

SKULLABONES
ISLAND

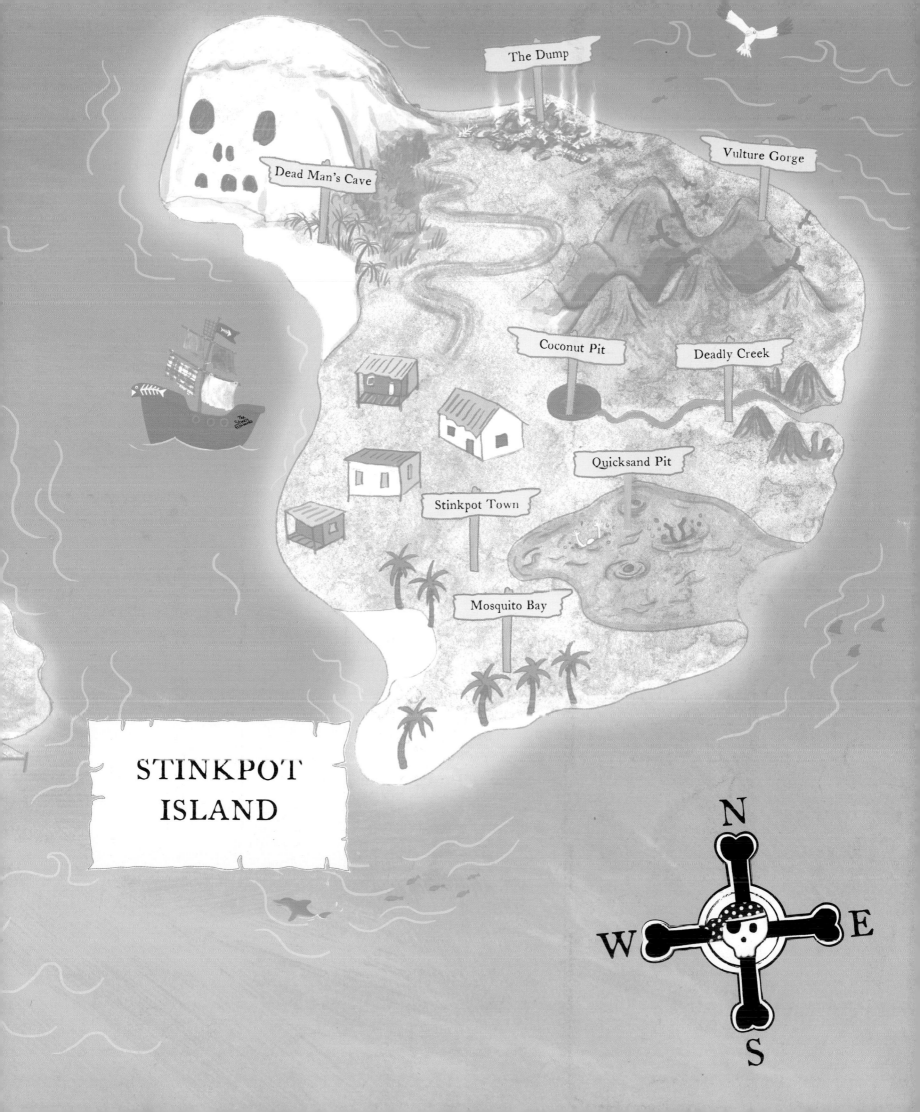

The Dump

Vulture Gorge

Dead Man's Cave

Coconut Pit

Deadly Creek

Quicksand Pit

Stinkpot Town

Mosquito Bay

STINKPOT
ISLAND

N

W   E

S